Let's DO EVERYTHING and NOTHING

JULIA KUO

Roaring Brook Press

New York

Will you climb a hill with me?

Dive into a lake with me?

Read the starry sky with me

and watch the clouds parade?

We'll scale the highest snowy peak,

we'll gasp at creatures of the deep.

We'll follow trails on summer nights

and salute majestic beasts.

Will we reach the very top,

the very bottom,

the very end?

We will.

We'll share the quiet twilight hour.

We'll find our path down step-by-step.

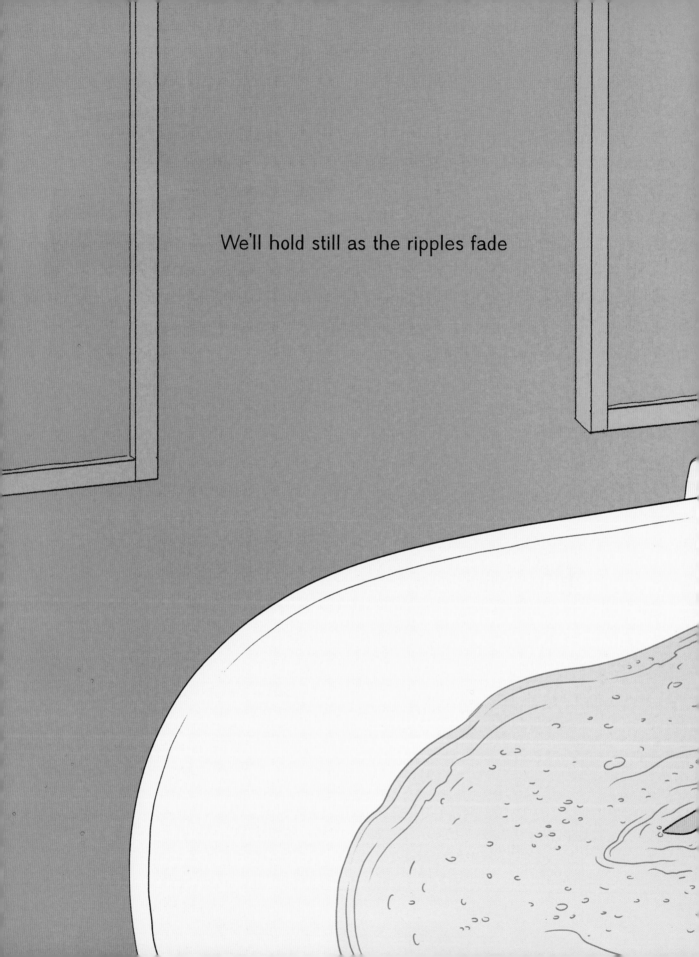

We'll hold still as the ripples fade

and watch the shadows stretch.

We'll rest,

we'll doze,

we'll be.

We'll do everything

and nothing,

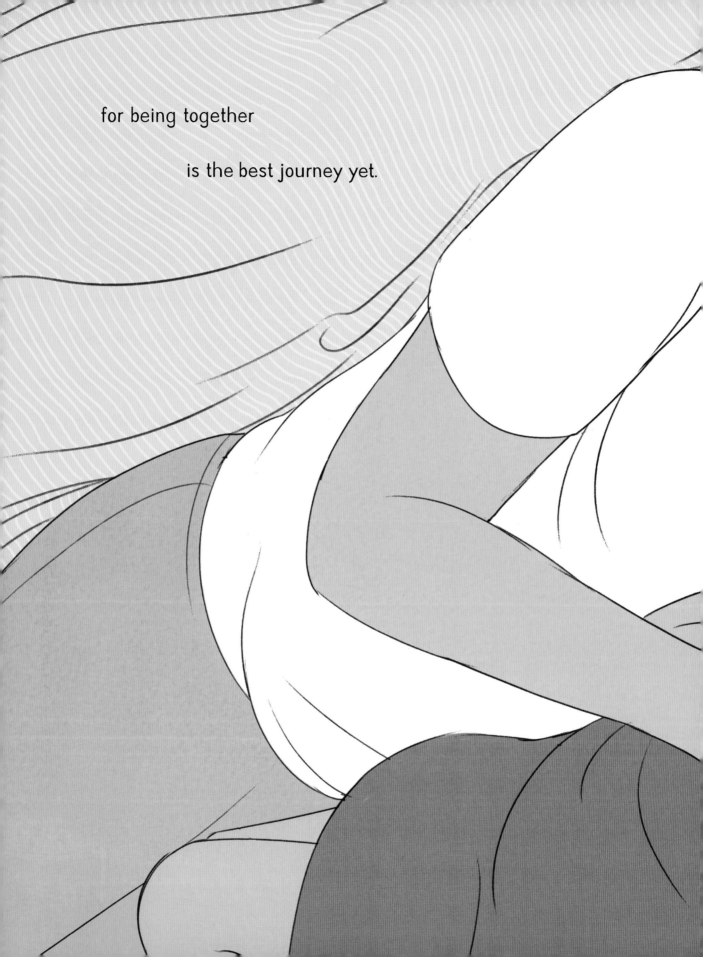

for being together

is the best journey yet.

To A–
for adventure, home, and everything in between

ABOUT THE BOOK

The illustrations were created digitally in Adobe Photoshop, and the text was set in YWFT Absent Grotesque. This book was edited by Connie Hsu, art directed by Jen Keenan, and designed by Mercedes Padró. The production manager was Susan Doran, and the production editor was Avia Perez.

Published by Roaring Brook Press
Roaring Brook Press is a division of Holtzbrinck Publishing Holdings Limited Partnership
120 Broadway, New York, NY 10271 • mackids.com

Library of Congress Cataloging-in-Publication Data is available.
ISBN 978-1-250-77434-7

Our books may be purchased in bulk for promotional, educational, or business use. Please contact your local bookseller or the Macmillan Corporate and Premium Sales Department at (800) 221-7945 ext. 5442 or by email at MacmillanSpecialMarkets@macmillan.com.

First edition, 2022
Printed in China by Toppan Leefung Printing Ltd., Dongguan City, Guangdong Province

1 3 5 7 9 10 8 6 4 2